Liberty
And
The Tall Mouse
By
A. Foster
Aka Ann Foster, Annette Foster

We have been in a "lock down" for approximately six weeks. For some of us it has even been longer.
We will not let this win.
We are soldiers in a war.
We never left home.
We were invaded.

When we finally get to come out of our cages,
life will not be the same.

It will never be the same.

The word or rather phrase:
Social Distance
will come to haunt all of us.

"They" will continue to try and take our humanity.

<u>We can not let them!</u>

What have we learned from this ordeal?

We need to be more aware of what is happening.
Not just here in our country, but all over the world.
We need to be more self sufficient.
We need to be less dependant on anyone else.
We need to remember what it was to be American.

God
Family
Country

We need to remember who we are.
We need to become: America(n) again!

Pray and lift up all that you love.
for if He is with you…
None can stand against you!

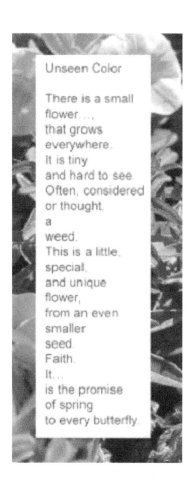

Unseen Color

There is a small
flower…,
that grows
everywhere.
It is tiny
and hard to see.
Often, considered
or thought,
a
weed.
This is a little,
special,
and unique
flower,
from an even
smaller
seed.
Faith.
It…
is the promise
of spring
to every butterfly.

This is a work of fiction.
Names, characters, places, and incidents
are the products of the author's imagination only.

"Again, this is a work of fiction.
Names, characters, places, and incidents
are the products of the author's imagination
or are used "fictitiously".
Any resemblance to actual events,
locales, or persons, living, dead,
mistaken for dead,
or undead,
is
entirely
coincidental."

No part of this book is meant to be offensive.
Free speech is important and can sometimes be
unwelcome. But should always be allowed, written,
spoken, and heard in order for their to be peace..

Thank you.

All things worth doing,
begin with Him!

This book is dedicated to all the weak…
and the abused…
trapped by this disaster,
in unsafe places.

Jesus protect them.
Please…

Amen.

Free Books!
BooksbyAFoster.com

A short note to say
Thank you for supporting a
true dreamer.

God Bless!

Just laughing…
    because we can!

Crying…
    When we have no choice left.

This book was given to:

_____

_____

_____

_____

_____

By:

_____

_____

_____

_____

_____

Note:

_____

_____

_____

_____

_____

*God Bless America
and all those who stand & protect her
forever!*

Table of Contents

The Bill of Rights, belongs to all of us.
Do not be in a hurry to let even a small part
be twisted or changed

The Red Letters

They stand out in the bible,
because they are the very word of God.
Pay attention.
Don't miss anything more.
You may need to know this stuff later.
When there are far fewer people,
to help you.

They are selling off our resources
to foreign lands like there is no tomorrow;
because there is not going to be one,
unless we wake up in time to say, "no".
There will be great changes,
and few will believe they are real.
Even when they are presented to them;
in public and before all others.

Cheaters and eaters of the day,
wasting away thinking about tomorrow…
that will not come, at all.
Mice, rats, small creatures…
that eat things no one else wants,
to find out they have great value.

But not again…
to anyone that matters.
only the small,
that want to be tall…
after all.

Free,
Until they knock down the door…
and then…

Poems

1) One Nation Under God

From sea to shining sea,
manifest destiny.
Every American third grader,
from 1960 and before,
could recite all the most important facts,
and tell you every score.
That is when they really taught, "school".
No one was a fool.

Everyone was blessed who got to go.
It was a big deal... freedom, and rights!
We wore our best clothes,
and tried to prepare.
(God, Family, Country!)

There were those that had, "less".
There were some with "much".
The common thread in Our flag...
we were all equal.

My classroom had every color,
and not the rainbow flag.
It had real kids,
with everyday problems,
and
dreams of growing up in a land,
loved and respected
around the world.

Yet the people now;
they mock and laugh,
and say it is a gaff...!
To respect and stand,
and lend a hand,
and be more than...

...and not less.

2)

Commenting on the Weather

My coffee is hot,
the cream was cold,
the outcome... just right.
The screen,
the window out and into the world...
awaits my thoughts and dreams,
to take me places I have never seen.

In my passing I am gifted,
to be allowed to read the poems of others.
I humbly leave remarks to cheer them on.
But it is I,
who am cheered and given hope,
not just for my self,
but for all that I know,
or will come to know.

While the categories,
call to some parts of me...,
pieces of my personality,
I try to write well.
Then in turn I find a sweet time,
that I can cherish those artists,
lost and found...
children of both war and peace.
Their hearts not on their sleeves,
but on white living paper.
It moves...
from person to person,
creating waves of
emotions,
to swing back...
for and against the tide.

All gathered together... to speak.
Free to say things,
whispered and loud.
Thankful,
ever for the privilege
and freedom,
bought and paid for
by others...
in a rain, (reign)
of blood.

3) Wisdom For A Coin

The essence of honesty in action,
a kind word, a special moment.
Many walk on by,
and do not even try.

The division of our country,
is not for or against,
it is the lack of God in all aspects.
At the dinner table,
around the clock,
we favor what is easy and "woke".
But the reality of tomorrow,
is that the lies of today,
spume-ed freely out;
in the media,
and over the net...
will be written on the walls,
of purgatory,
for those left to make sure
they are never forgotten.
Sadly only to find out,
there is no such thing...
and they are forever in hell.

What is "it" that we say,
what we speak,
what we breathe?
That has importance to someone,
barely listening?
If it is not a truth,
the emotion is a lie.
You need to remember that.
Or in the end,
when you are left,
and there is no one...
but,
them;
there will be no place,
to run, or hide or even die.

It is your only "hope".

4) The Crowned Dead

The growing of green things,
should concern all of us.
The fires burning in far lands,
can still reach US(a).
There are all kinds of flames.
Not all are hot, some are ice cold.
They drive you to run into the sea,
even as it boils.

Fear of toxicity,
and death by chemical cast-offs,
or delinquent occurrences of stupidity.
The world is slipping closer
to the orbit set at the beginning of time.
Prophesied and foretold,
to the level of awareness,
none will or can be naive.
The plain sight of news,
media playing games,
tiny titans of power...
bereft of might,
and liberty used as a weapon.
The enemies at the door.

Sky buses full of horse droppings,
fraudulent reasons to spread chaos,
further among the peasants...
staring into their TV's for signs,
"They" do not want seen.

What are the number of the sick?
Have you seen the cities of the dead?
They are vacant and made of concrete,
that crack(s) from lack of zoning requirements.
Tainted miss-shape-en causes,
to focus not on the Light of tomorrow,
but the darkness of today.

Is this a mirror of what you dished out?
Have you killed others to build your world,
upon theirs?
Beware.

5) Wormwood

There is a place,
in the middle of nowhere... now. (hushed whisper)
It is hot and cooking,
and yet...things are green.
Nature has taken back,
what man destroyed.
Maybe not the way it should be,
but maybe it does not matter,
or it is too late an affair.
She has pushed past the evil,
in favor of...
We are yet,
to know for sure.

Yes, there are animals,
many but not the same.
The weak ones died.
The strong became stronger.
They became smarter, faster.
More clever, more aware.

Butterflies vanished.
Bees... small grains of sand
blown away.

The people were told to leave.
Many, even most did.
Some if not all returned,
the ones that had nowhere else,
to go.
Of them,
many died as well.
Again the invalids were weaned away,
and the mighty became better,
or at least less than dead.

What can be said for this place?
An accident waiting to happen...still.
As it already took place, and will again.
The concrete tomb is breaking down,
and evil is trying to crawl out from below.
From beneath the rock that man sat upon its face.
Brave heroes now are trying to fight,
what can only be heard.
A song of cancer and disease,
change to everything that was,
to something that is
and will be until the end.

The angel stands still...
a simple statue and tribute to the loss,
blowing the horn of warning,
now decades past.

How is time measured?
Not in moments of hesitation,
but souls gathered before the feast.
All the clocks have stopped,
a burst in the atmosphere.
So many still walking among the dead,
already corpses themselves,
unaware they have been
radiated not once,
but repeatedly...

6) Gathering the Bones

You must believe me,
I am in power.
I know what is right for you.
Your vote put me here,
you can not possibly be wrong?
You have too much pride for that.
I have been here now,
nearly forever. (years and years without limit)
So what is the difference?

Not to fear,
they redrew the lines to make sure,
only last year.
It... will work exactly as it should.
Near the cemetery,
to allow for voter confidence
and the column to other places...
far from here that hate US(a) the most,
a funnel to new spaces that "I" okay,
to train...
to take over...
what they can not
just raze.

I am moral and ethical.
I believe in "free" for all.
Unlimited medical and dental,
all you can eat education...
until the teachers quit from lack of pay.
Open places to live in all new buildings,
to be happy and well cared for,
by the middle,
until it too is hollowed out
gutted, for bait to chum for sharks.
It is okay...

pee anywhere you like.
Someone will be along shortly,
to wipe it up...
or not.

I stand for life,
the pro-"life" of my bank account.
the advance of my wages and pension,
the money I will make on the name,
and those of my family...
to be rich.
I will jump on jets and go where I like,
and you will be left to walk...
and talk about days gone.
Vote on...
like you mean it,
as it will not matter.
That too has been fixed ahead.
So you, and you, and you...
will behind.

Thank you, I guess,
you have a "use" after all.

Open the gates and let the world...
come inside.
I don't have to live near them,
you have provided for much better,
to care for all my needs,
and feeds.

Let "them" kill the Citizens.
Let "them" rule the land.
It is okay,
as "I" am in command.

(The many faces of death,
the visage of darkness grows... in plain sight.)

7) The Fever Spreads

I am slipping.
Not slowly but faster than expected.
I wanted it to go better.
I made a plan and have a goal.
It has not worked out.

Writing, penning, grinning...
Crying, sighing, and not dying.
Words, dancing across my desk on fire.
Some have already drowned,
and I have not even filled my glass,
with wine or water.

Emotions doing battle,
laughing and swimming on a lake,
somewhere else...
not here.
"Come back,
and take me... with you."

A feather out of ink,
a quill without blood,
to spare the wicked and the good,
from boredom.
Flicking boogers,
eating crickets, and wondering
how many people are waiting at the door,
of the cell, they have put me in?

Are the walls made of brick and mortar,
or even paper... like the tigers in china,
that come in many colors,
and have no teeth to bite,
only gums to chew...?
The few remaining pieces of my brain,
left after the party,
that should have taken place,
at the docks,
have pooled together,
and become a new species of wild animal,
trying to get out of the cage.
Oh my, worse yet...
this is beginning to make sense.

8) Tyrants Walk

What shall I feed my children?
The garden is empty,
the plants have been pulled up.
The dog, we ate already.
There are no rats in the traps.
Instead, they live in the palace,
where the fence is live wire,
and the guns shoot the chickens,
begging for scraps or seed.

People that know no hunger,
and have never known pain,
can not decide for me or you,
what is to be gained.
By losing the very boundaries...
of our nation,
giving room for the wild to roam,
will do more not less,
toward bringing about
 the beginning of the end.

Revelations re-read,
and sadly re-written,
a sin to be paid for at the gate.
The fate of the marked,
and the willingness to sell early...
for the right price,
to grow readily the wealth,
of momentary desire.

Buying the country for a price,
sold to the highest bidder,
retaking the house that belongs...
not to them, but to the people,
by crazy undead, living beyond the grave,
vicariously alive through
the body parts of the young...
stolen in the night,
children of another faith.

Are you tall, are you short?
What color is your skin?
Is the material you are made of...
useful?
Are there too many of you?

Creepy governments lending a hand,
terrorists worshiped for their leadership skills,
in killing the young and innocent.
Stop the insanity of Orwell's predictions,
the flood too great for the dam.

Yell out,
wolves among sheep,
riddles in the dark,
New York City Park,
The scarecrow screams,
"Hark!"
"Who goes there?"

The devil has appeared in plain sight,
it is time to fight, it is too late to flee.
There is nowhere to go.

9) The Worth of Rice

Food is a daily need.
Some eat well, are fed well,
are taken care of,
while others have little,
or none.

It is what we do with what we have,
that is the difference between,
living and living well.
The quality of life,
ever the goal to be higher...
than expected of,
or made to.
To have a price,
un-payable...
except by Him,
who had no need of money,
and yet was betrayed for silver.
The sad seller in the transaction,
hanged in the bargain,
to live forever among "them",
in the dark.

Sacrifices have a thousand faces,
from time spent to cash lost.
Blood given, missed moments,
and abuse.
Loss, and grief, the brothers of regret,
in the end the mirror of our lives,
everything that was bought and sold,
that made a difference,
between the line of gray...
and the deep of black.

BooksbyAFoster.com

10) High Powered Fences

Beyond Your Vote

Armchair Politian's sitting beside Ceasar(a),
believing or at least making believe...
that they are for the people,
and not against.
"They" have been there too long.
Rot is strong, coming from the corpses.

They point thin-sharp fingers,
and makeup rules,
using the tools, of the trade.
Lies like snakes,
that live on both land and water,
in every form of underling,
pressed into service...
for the queen, of nothing.

Lowlife voters pleading for honesty,
from dark web media that has sold out.
The land-turtles living in office,
fighting over the scraps of the victory garden,
a warning of war already in the distance.
Like bugs eating their own fallen,
while striving to start a new colony,
they chant over the electric lines...
martyr-ism.
Of a hero, no, of a monster.
How is lifting evil up okay?
If not backed by the lies of a religion,
as dark as those that hide their face,
like cowards do,
and bow.

You have read it at the end of every book.
It is the same sunrise and sunset.
It is just another day,
no matter what the media say.

They scream and yell and cry,
like Hinny Penny and the Sky.
The facts quit... not quite the case.
The prayers of a country,
saints gathered knowing all are coming.
Standing up for the weak,
taking back and remembering.
Waking up the old to dance again...
on the government franchise,
we should own from the illegal gotten gain,
the children of the political elite,
and supreme, cheerleaders of the third world.

The larks in the media,
busy telling us...
all they want us to know.
The reality is "they" do their best business,
lying to us all.
There will be an accounting.
There will be, a fall.
The time is coming.
That is the call.

11)

America by the Square Foot

We here in this part of the country,
love God and stand for the flag.
We here in this part of the country,
honor the military,
help widows and orphans...
and tar and feather,
lowlife liars,
posing as Politian's,
for the betterment
of erasing all things
worth believing in
or standing up for.

If you want to know my state,
my county, my city or town,
it is not far from where you live.
Where you have taken up residence,
behind walls that we paid for,
and think we will be okay,
with continuing to dish out cash to,
as you put US(a) out into the streets,
covered with the dung of humans.
Creating new jobs in your neighborhood,
is to apply for the cleanup squad.
They should have called the
Ghostbusters,
and consumed the ectoplasm that has
invaded ALL of the golden state,
taking away its shine forever.

Read your history,
silly rich folk.
It did not go well for the elite of
Europe,
as they fell to plague and disaster,
at the hands of their own stupidity,
now repeated...
embracing leprosy,
typhus,
hepatitis,
measles,
and the new sickness,
racism and hypocrisy rampant...
among the elite,
currently in office.

God

takes care

of every bird.

12) Crazy

Mental Health aka Crazy

The very topic is inclusive of the word,
that haunts our every step from birth;
until our last breath.

Fear has no power except that which we give it.
Knowing that we are all passing away,
every day of our lives;
leaves us closer to the tomorrow we are putting off.
It is here and at our door,
in front of us now.

Bucket lists and things to do.
Suddenly no paper to write them down.
No items yet attained now unattainable;
changes without notice.
Hearts skip,
tests come back wrong.
It matters not at all the rhyme or reason,
only that the season has changed.

Memory fades.
Loved ones with cancer.
Victim or caregiver...
the outcome of damage reflective only
in the ultimate loss of all that dreams meant.

Bipolar, skizo, opioids and mary j...
Desperate for a normality which never actually existed.
The truth of our continuation...
a relationship with God.
As only He;
is yesterday,
today,

13) Stop Killing My Country

Accused of political banter,
to speak the words, God Bless,
and America in the same sentence.
Bespeaking the fear,
of being proud,
just to be born in a land free from tyranny.
Where anyone can still be more...
than they were,
before they got here,
for the price of a ticket.
and a stamp,
a dream to be better than all others,
to stand together,
for something greater than self.

Words of hate and surreal punishments
given by the overly offended for nothing more,
then the disagreement that all fires are hot,
or at least...
the ones we start
and the ones we can not...
put out.

What clarity would you request of the new year,
that you could not see before now?
The year itself, 2020.
Plain and perfect sight,
historically, and for our future...
all of us.

What chance at a life without pain and death,
at the whim of someone that does not even...
now your name,
or that you exist?

Tyrants that hide behind small rockets.
Afraid of face powder and lipstick,
building empty cities, to make-believe,
in their own world.

Convincing their populace,
they are okay...
living in the dark.
Deathly fearful, they will find out,
the truth...bleeding through the air,
the atmosphere of deceit,
clearing slowly,
regardless of the efforts,
pressed and molded by the black.

Others building in even larger zones...
of emptiness,
Ruled by heartless human haters,
dividers between those that have...
and those that have not,
putting their trash into the ocean,
making their problem yours,
ours and not theirs at all.
Cheating their own people...
out of living.
Putting some in prisons,
to harvest,

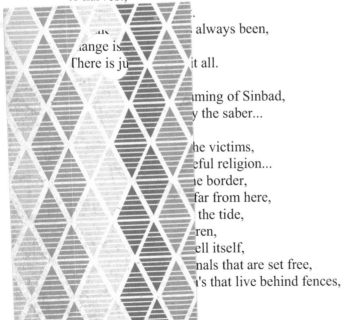

always been,
.ange is
There is ju   it all.

                    iming of Sinbad,
                    y the saber...

                    he victims,
                    eful religion...
                    ie border,
                    far from here,
                    the tide,
                    ren,
                    ell itself,
                    nals that are set free,
                    i's that live behind fences,

41

and get paid for doing nothing more...
then tearing down the country,
by its very basic and historic foundations.

Forefathers pacing the halls of heaven,
speaking words we can not hear.
The flag still waving in spite of the best efforts,
of those using OUR OWN Freedoms,
given to all, too stab and kill,
with zest.

If you can not abide by the rules,
if you have no desire to bend the knee...
or assimilate and call this your home,
"In God We Trust" interregnal to the premise,
of all men are created equal...
please feel free to return to whatever country,
is free'er,
kinder,
nicer,
gentler,
and above all safer...
than the very one,
you live in now.

Then...
Shout your obscenities from the prisons,
of your own land,
where you would face,
torture and death,
for the words you freely cast,
out upon those that gave you peace,
and the hand of acceptance.

America

from

Sea to Shinning Sea

14) Bigger than You Think

The internet,
is large... indeed.
It starts here and never ends.
It just starts over somewhere else.

In the beginning AOL,
time spent waiting to connect.
Now we sail across the sea,
and stream everything from you...to me.

It is illusive and right in front,
it is scary and beautiful,
intelligent and stupid...
like a woman you first met,
at a place, you would not dare go back to,
and found she followed you home,
wants to marry you and has already taken,
your I.D.

Welcome Mrs. Smith,
glad you decided to return.
Will it be the formal suite?
at the cost,
more money than my account
could ever afford, or I could ever earn,
on a good day, much less a bad.
Then the bank calls and tells me,
my account is overdrawn,
and my license has been denied.
I want to hide, but I can not,
snail mail, email, first impressions,
and half baked...
the cake has been sitting out too long.

I can send a package to New York,
costs me less to Africa,
if I send it via China.
Has anyone else noticed this circle,
except the man taking my money?
He has an odd and knowing smile,

on his visage.
What inner secret does he have,
how can I get part of that?

You tube, my new teacher:
I can fix my dryer and make bread.
I can also spend or spent,
untold hours watching things,
I should never have see.
Worse yet connected to games,
that win nothing,
but take everything,
I have remaining...
willingly,
if absently given.

Now I understand,
they can see me as well?
How is that possible.
Why would they want to look?
Who are they?
My list in this area,
is rather long...

Media giants taking turns with their toys,
playing and ever hitting them together,
to make strange sounds.
It is our right to choose the news,
or so they say,
until there is no country,
to have rights in, anymore.
All lost by people living out their idealism,
instead of standing together as a nation.
As one,
As one against the tide,
the rising tide of black, that covers
like cancer on a screen where it is
tolerant of drugs,
but not accepted by them,
or the people that use them.

Amazon, we deliver.
A miracle of the times.

I am not for or against,
that would be like breathing,
once the ball has dropped.
At least by appearance you are aware,
of all those that stare,
at your wealth, jealous of your success,
yet, you laugh in their face and provide jobs,
all need desperately.
(except in New Your where you are valued less)

This now...
is the willingness of our time -
to sell out humanity,
in favor of Borg technology.
Once we have been assimilated,
it will feel more centered,
and less sidelined,
by football heroes that never,
leave their chairs.

Text on my friends,
although against the law.
It is our right to run people over,
that do not,
get out of the way.
some say.
But they are few
and less conscious of reality...
as a whole.
Most are unsure as to which stall,
to put their head in,
and which to take their minds off,
in order to be correct...
for now.

Heroes in churches,
standing their ground,
pounding the darkness back.
Proving that the agenda
we are fed, is full of flies and lies,
by people in power.
Trying to take away,
all that they can,

to give to those that have none,
but willing to take,
even what is not theirs,
and never was.

Prayers is the order of the day,
unless you feel you can make it,
alone.
In that case,
I will pray for you,
you will need it.

15)

Cyrus

President of the country,
not like any that came before.
Or... Like any that will follow.
Standing in the gap between the flood,
and the waters of eternity,
threatening to consume the weak,
kill the innocent,
and feast on the unwary.
The man was voted in by the people,
but clearly printed in the word,
his name; a Trumpet... of His Coming!

Your hand Sir, held high,
a pen, sword, a law to be made,
a few to be broken,
that should have never...
been written at all.
Blessings on you, your family,
all those that serve the righteous
cause of the Lord's plan.

The military might of Moses,
winning by the hand of GOD...
against the chariots of Pharaoh.
No obstacle before you, beside you, or...
behind you, will pull you down,
as you hold Israel high!
God's blessed land...
God's blessed people!

Killing off the minions of darkness,
in sweeping storms of truth.
Draining the alligators,
the crocodiles, and tiny slimy sucker fish...
from the swamps of our country,
in order to prepare better fields of green.
A glory to God on the highest!

Prayers to you, Sir.
Prayers to your family.
You hug our flag in your arms,
like you hold something dear.
There is no fear left in the land,
only the echoing sound(s)...
of the Horn,
the Horn of Jubilee!

16)

The Fact(s)

It started with a poem.
Penned in by mistake.
Then it ended up in a letter,
that later turned into an email.
That was forwarded,
not once but a thousand,
and then ten million times.

Then someone was asked,
what it all meant.
They were floored by the fact,
no one knew.
But some did,
and some took action.
Some gathered,
while others spent.
Some prayed,
will others chose to laugh.

Respectful of no one,
nothing is as it was,
and the old have no bones,
left to gnaw.
Awaken the lazy child,
staying in the basement...
living on the meat sized portion,
of the daily bread,
at the discretion of their
own parents,
busy making a living,
before they die.

A level field of uncommon valor,
that has no heroism in it at all.
One no better the next,
cogs in the wheels...
of a larger machine.
Then broken and left,
beside the road,
rotting...
on their way,
to nowhere.

17) Strange Weather

The camels are swimming,
and who knew...
they knew how?
What a surprise...
to all that stood by,
watching them cross the desert,
like ducks on a pond.

Careful and fearful,
some should be,
as the sucking sand,
has grown hungry.
Pulling the unwary down,
to a breathless grave.

Why are the skies above,
raining down with such violence?
Why are we the receivers,
of such a storm of strength...?
Surely, nothing to do,
with the mocking,
that has been done,
at the fountains...
and wells of God.

Fires in lands, that thirst.
With no hope of deluge,
to succor their souls?
Further eastward still...
in other lands,
the plagues are loose,
in the stands.
High rises full of death,
to mock the power,
they wish to steal.
But could never hope...
to understand,
much less wield.

The Jubilee has sounded.
The years are counting off.
Measure your futures,
not by death,
but by the clock of forever.
It will tick by as...
you will live,
to sing, or grieve...
eternally.

18) Dangerous Visions

I see you and you see me.
We are not free anymore.
Or at least that is your intent.
You place the bonds...
you brought with you,
on all that will willingly take them...
However, you are about to find,
that there are still some,
in fact many,
that will not.

Our flag is important...
to US(a). All of US(a).
Do not stomp on her colors.
They do not run,
they fight.

No assimilation;
as it will be met with a force,
greater than expected.
Stronger than determined
possible, by deplorable,
underlings.

We don't want your ways.
We have our own.
They are not perfect,
but they are... Ours!
That is why,
every country in the world,
wants to be like us,
wants to be us.

Their citizens are starving,
they are unsafe.
They are crying,
about death and mutilations,
over religions that kill,
by the force of a dark will,
not even their own.

Wake up!
Our country sets you free.
That is the promise of this land.
Race, creed and color,
a story that is still being written,
even as they fight...
to erase it from existence.

Stronger by far,
a group of unlikely patriots,
that feel deeply about their families,
their Country
and their God.
Everyday citizens...
that have found,
true connection,
with what is,
and was important,
Freedom.

19) No War

In the days...
between here and there,
many will find,
time for reflection.
Time to consider...
all that was lost,
all that was gained,
everything worth keeping,
all things worth forgetting.

In the end,
the embrace of the New Year...
the hope of tomorrow.

Cheering,
crying,
and laughing at everything.
You, me, we,
need to remember,
and have not let others
forgive.

Gather your families close.
Be happy, we are not socialists.
We have a dream,
that is still possible,
for every man, woman,
and child.

America,
She is beautiful.
Her people steady,
because of the rock,
Our God,
We Trust!

Soldiers come home,
we are at peace.

20)

A Statement

When I was young,
my Aunt burned her braw.
She fought for rights,
for me, and my daughter(s),
that I had no idea,
I did not have.

Voting,
equal pay,
the chance to say,
what is important.
A woman's view,
to add a lighter touch,
to partisan screams.
Sadly only human,
not always right,
not always wrong.

Graceful dedication,
to the truth about our land.
We the people,
together we stand.

The right to vote,
and make a difference,
important to one and all.
Citizens that feel the same,
about freedom,
and the lack of it.

21) Run Through in Babylon

Friends, I wish to speak,
but they have cut out my tongue.
So I fumble...

Instead,
I hear your words, they are strong,
and your passion true.
However, it is the content of which,
I would have stated my thoughts,
provoked from despair,
into a desperate plea.
Against you...
against me.
But and always...
against them.

In the streets on the corner,
"ganda" is talked up,
(propaganda: made up facts by those in power,
to promote even greater strength by deceit.)
about everything that is bad
and happening less than perfect,
in the world.
Tiny Kong is beaten to a pulp,
citizens torn apart in the streets,
for meat,
for potatoes,
and for organs eaten by the rich,
and elegant of taste.

The east, far from here,
they kill and murder Christians,
Jews and saints with equal vigor.
There is no reason to tell them apart,
or upset the apple cart.
Deals made in the dark,
by sold out government traitors,
sworn to their own cause,
without pause for effect,
to the green deal,
or the appeal to the lower class.

I watch TV, and wince at the news.
Lies mixed with spices...
to feel and look the way they...
want us to be, not free.
Spewing words,
not truth,
but stranger than fiction.
It is a holy war,
unseen in the shadows,
complete in the darkness,
and living in plain sight.

"They" kill babies,
and make laws against the sick,
the poor and the legal.
The last on the list to be attended,
and the first to be helped to the grave.
Who are "they"?

I read the factions on both sides.
What I want to hear,
solutions and timely possibilities,
that would ease the suffering of all.
I don't care about Russia,
they are crooks or not...
I don't care about Ukraine,
it is a pain.

If their are bad men holding office,
or have ever held,
they should be brought to justice,
made to "pay for play",
back to the Americans
they lied too.

Your political time tables,
are all running out.
We the people are ready to shout.
Do something for us,
stop being against,
one way or the other,
someone will be...
impaled on the fence.

22)

Fear of Acceptance

The queen called her jester,
and requested a joke!
He had nothing to say,
He just sat there,
as he had already choked.

Nonsense was delivered,
to the king of the land...
to the shock and surprise
of every grown man.
Sane and insane,
Drugged just the same.

Shout out for freedom,
Until it is heard...
Beyond the borders of
stupidity...
Sung in every foreign nation,
before the tyrants,
and elite can grasp
the peasants have gained
a foothold into and onto;
a world
level and counted...
Not in dollars and cents,
but in flags,
of the True Prince.
The Lord of Righteousness,
The Holy King.

God's beauty seen

in every sunrise and sunset!

23) State Glamour

Bright beautiful colors,
brilliant, not halfway.
That is the fair,
the beautiful fair.
It is in the air...

The smells of sweet potatoes,
dipped in chocolate and fried,
until someone cried.
Fruits and nuts are king.
The cows and bulls,
the judges...no fools,
first place to the chickens.
They are the most accommodating,
regardless of color, or accent.

Ferris wheels,
and fast-moving rides,
that hide the agenda of the skeptics,
tired of cleaning up, the party.
The ones that should have stayed home,
and can not ever be left alone,
as they fall apart,
when placed upon the apple cart.

A New Year,
to give us new numbers,
for our fancy calendars.
While some take things away,
as they can, to lead all astray.
Let us remember the fun,
we all had, as one,
in the sun of a new day,
a new way,
to lift up each other,
and give back,
more than we take,
in the wake,
of hope itself.

24) Our Flag Waved

Written by: Ann Foster

Our Flag Waved
in a foreign land...

Given the taste,
of sweet,
savory, freedom...
The people cry out for more.
Scared they are about to be,
mummified forever,
in the throng of one-ness.

Your pretty faces,
will be ugly and all just alike.
You will conform to the proper,
hair-do...
You will dress in what we give you,
wear what you must,
and above all...
die as "We" see fit.

It will not happen quickly...
no-not fast at all.
We want to make an example.
Do not fear or shed a tear,
no one will hear you scream.
Organs gifted to the rich,
bought and sold to the highest.

No...
we will not eat you all today,
we have to do it slowly,
so it will last.

Your children,
we will take,
and give each one a chance,
to dance in the darkness...
of illiteracy,
and ensure our path to glory,
is a long and golden road.

Like the great wall,
filled with bodies,
our land is full of ghosts,
hosts for the unwilling
and hatred of all things free.

25) Thief of Glory

Faded flowers,
dead on the table,
no vase, no water,
no blood,
no sacrifice,
of time, sweat, tears,
years and fears.

Regardless of the race,
unable to meet the rules,
making up your own,
to go along.
The crowd too busy to notice,
you are too big for your britches,
too tall for your crown,
too wanting in your desire,
to lead the parade.
Willing to step on...
the innocence of hope,
eating and relishing,
magnificence unearned.

Yea... that they call your name,
in praise and yet future retribution,
of all that you have stolen,
and can not give back.
Your sickness,
confusion of displacement,
a chance to be all that you are,
and taking more not less from others,
to achieve your purpose,
a splendor in the garden...
of white roses,
stained to red.

When you count your trophies,
and see the symbols of fame,
remember it is your name,
that came before all others.
That was important at the time,
and less so now.
But it is too late to change,
a history of destruction,
"Self Preservation",
far more worthy a title,
then "Queen" of anything.

Truly in the end,
a king of nothing.

26) The Carcass

The best part of the meal,
the bones, the things others throw away.
The wingtips, the neck, the gizzard, the lizard...
a fowl needs to be cooked and stewed.

A bit of broth, a giant onion, scallions if you have them.
Carrots because they are bright orange...
Celery, long stalks, and short,
for the picky and tough eaters.

Simmer and boil, worth the effort,
like friendship and the kitchen sink.
It makes you question,
"Why do good cooks have so many friends?"
The answer plain and apparent.
They know how to roll dough and make bread.
Both having nothing to do with money.
Yet worth more than a fortune,
to all that need to eat,
all who are hungry.

Chicken noodle, turkey steak,
pork chops and wine in a cave,
held by the rich, while the poor starved.
Buying the votes of the country,
(is it for sale? has it already been sold?)
while holding us/it hostage...
for the holidays.

The New Year gives US(a) promises,
maybe no one can keep.
Black-eyed peas are sold out,
at the store,
in case you want more,
than before.
There will be less for all,
if they change the law,
and no president,
will ever be free...
and for the people...
again.

27)

Strong Voices

Strong Voices, Fixed Opinions.

"Bashing",
the political warfare,
of the uncommon man.
The rights of all those in power,
ungodly "saints"...
that walk on higher ground,
to prove they are better than the rest.

Alienated and disturbed...
by the fact,
we put them there,
on top of the world.
Famous for all the wrong things.
Not for saving people,
or heroic acts,
but for keeping the small,
ever smaller.

Eat your dogs,
and say little,
that is what is expected of you,
and you and you and you.
We are your betters,
and fretters best beware,
or we will quietly send you...
down the stair.

Some heads will role,
some broke the law,
more are far above it still.
While others, only tried to call out
the ragged edges for what they were...
or are... or will be.

Bad words they speak,
while we dine at the 5:00 o'clock hour.
Pressing their agenda,
into our faces,
until we can not eat...
anymore.

28)

When Freedom Grows Cold

(not a nice poem)

One day the dogs will not bark.
I/we will not be ready,
as they will have failed...
to do all that was needed,
and asked of them.
Perhaps not their fault,
as in Venezuela...
they are eaten by the poor.
There are a lot of hungry, there.
Not so many dogs, anymore.

At church, we fold dollars,
with funny pictures,
of past and present rulers,
unimportant now.
Once hailed high in that foreign land,
now laid low by socialism,
and "FREE for ALL".
Basically worthless colors,
to make butterfly bookmarks,
small angels to fly from tome to tome,
and hail the dangers of censorship,
the lack of freedom to discuss ideas...
freely from both sides of the fence,
fake news and propaganda,
one in the same,
a mirror into manipulation.
Built from the bones of the sad,
and the lost,
impaled on indecision...
once the high and the mighty.

Guns and violence given bad names,
bestowed as treason, and murder.
The truth, defendable land...
against tyrants and kings,
that pressure the weak into pits,
and shoot them for sport.

29)*Seasons of Abundance*

and Regret

Grandma was a farm cook,
never wasted a thing.
We ate good...
plain food.
She taught:
Never say words,
you will not eat,
as you can not leave them,
on your plate.
They will just stare at you,
until you wrap them up,
in a box,
go to the post office,
and send them to China.
There they have none.

Waste was a big thing,
in a house of plenty.
It was, and is, a bigger thing,
in a house of less.

Grandpa was a farmer,
later a construction man,
on big rigs and cats, not dogs.
He never swore and taught us all,
to read carefully,
listen well,
and never write anything down,
that we would not willing stand up
and say to all present.
As there may come a day,
we will be called to do just that,
for each other,

ourselves and our neighbors.
Who can't or won't take the mark,
as they know the meaning of the design,
and the flaw in the fabric.

30) Bad Discussions

(Not a nice poem)

By the pound what a sound,
in morbid delay at death's door.
Cutting off bits and chunks of souls,
too busy to be made whole.
Now withered on the blocks,
slaves to the lochs...
where things beneath the water,
must eat and cheat death,
for a day and a night,
and...
a day.

Sold withered youth,
a new battalion of the young,
under the rule of an order,
that echoes a foreign land.
A disaster of repeat potential,
the death of millions,
a blemish on the necktie;
of our history.
The hanging tree,
will readily accept all that
sign on,
and replace all that will not,
with chance passers-by.
They will be fed.

The rest...
will be dead.

The Fine Lady

It is the first time I can remember,
that I cared about china.
Which pattern to pick,
where to buy it,
and why.

The first ladies pick their dishes.
They pick special placements,
for the guests of the high house,
"the White House",
the people's house...
of this land.

Pretty patterns,
flowers, and trims...
to make the world a bit brighter.
Taking time to make everything,
perfect...
that represents;
our past,
present,
and future...

The values of our country,
freedom,
grace,
and honor...
loyalty
brothers beyond blood.

In God We Trust!
Values and morals that consider,
all while holding true to the roots,
or our forefathers.

Freedom.

32) Faraway Town

The problems of America,
they can not reach me.
I don't worry about a thing.
I live happily and free,
in the basement of my grandparent's house.

Why not my parents(?),
well they went to jail.
No, I live here for free.
They are afraid I will ask more,
but they should...
show me the door.

I am ungrateful,
I am a user prime,
to define my rights,
in other people's lives!

No boundaries,
no borders,
we are all alike.

Just because you hate us.
We must comply.
Tents at my front door,
sh.. in the street.
America a third world,
in a real-world,
of my own town.

No rule of law,
they can do as they please,
soon they will come
for you,
even if you have locks...
with keys.

You cry about debt, that you create.
You give away yours...and mine too.
No one said it was okay,
but it was politically correct.

Free education all around,
until there is no money,
to pay teachers,
that refuse to work without pay.

Free medical,
"come here for your hangnails",
let us pay for that,
we are so wealthy,
until we all fall flat.

Then there will be no service
for anyone, you or me or them.
Only those that can afford it,
that will be...mostly...
them.

America

Humble, because she is…

grateful to the Lord.

"In God We Trust"

Free… are her citizens.

Do not tread upon us!

33) Freedom's Last Cry

I do not agree...
with your personal views,
and prefer to avoid;
seeing them,
hearing them,
reading them.

It was just a choice,
not a judgment.
There is,
still freedom of choice,
until it too is gone,
with the rest.

No safe place.
No law and order.
No culpability,
and no responsibility.

When "we" are all silenced,
by the world view,
The Lion will roar,
and there will be true,
and real fear.
The Lamb that was slain,
will return.
Angels will sing,
and draw swords.
They will know their tasks,
and rush to do them.

Time a funny thing,
the blink of an eye,
the glint of a single tear,
year after year,
suddenly here!

President of Freedom

The last man in a long line,
voted to save the future...
for us.
Not all of us,
but some.

Those that live on others,
standing on the backs of oxen,
will get all that is theirs.

Unrelentingly working,
for a better tomorrow...
only to find some have been,
tied to a circle,
a pole in the ground.

Spending their days...
toiling and pulling,
pallets of overloaded,
waste products,
produced by the elected elite,
shoveled and force-fed
to the Deplorables...
all,
in an effort to make them...
choke and die.

Termites...
to eat the very nutrients...
from our trees.
Ants,
to consume...
what is not just leftover,
but all there is too eat.
Foul swine,
talked about in the bible,
and sent to drown.

The best man for the job,
was not the one
any would have picked,
first from the tree.
The apples of freedom
have been scarce.
Yet, one that loves America,
more than all the rest.
Clear and exactly what you see,
Our President is there to fight,
for you and me.

Higher wages,
safer homes,
better lives,
one legitimate vote away.
America is alive.
We are here to stay,
because we pray!

35) No

Denial.
I am not for,
I am not against,
I live...
setting on the fence.

I don't want to be involved,
I don't want to take a side,
I want to hide.
I want to be left alone,
I am not a bone.

Yes, I...
enjoy the right to choose.
I walk freely down the street.
No one comes to my home,
and beats me...
or takes my wife,
even if I want them too.

Yes, I...
make fun of everything,
your right to choose or die.
I want you to get along,
with every song,
from the other side.
Give away our land,
give away our money,
no borders and no laws,
that's... funny.

Someday impaled upon the fence,
that divided the isle between,
those that tell the truth,
and those that only mean...

High in the air,
dead to the world,
recycled,
into every day items
used by lost people.

The new third world,
the order,
the accepted tolerance level of dismissal.

Embrace the fact,
heaven's gate is beautiful.
Yet the distance from the fence line,
is ever to far from deaths door.

To die without a soul,
is to die forever empty of every dream.

The civil war was fought brother against brother,
father against son, and mothers and daughters cried...
and still cry.

One Nation
One Flag
One People

36) The Flag of Our Nation

Belongs to all that stand.
We hold together this land,
one person to another,
part of the fabric,
of all that we hold dear.

Red, White and Blue,
The colors never run!
They are known the world over.
Some fear, some should, some better.

Others need a hero.
Others need a hand.
It is what we stand for…
in this freedom land.

They want to come here,
every one of them...
There is no where like it,
in the world.
Some respect her,
others wish to tear her down.

Hear our hearts beat,
the sound grows louder,
as the elections draw nearer.

"We the people",
Stand up.
"We the people",
Take back what is ours.

This is my land,
This is your land,

This is America.
Amen.

37) Pass Trade

Do not waste more time!

It is fire and spit,
thin water and urine.
All lies from city folk.
The swamp smells,
it is dying.
No new water,
just the old cesspool inlets,
all the outlets, blocked.

Cockroaches running,
for the sides of the room,
but there is no trim…
to scurry beneath,
or under.
It has been removed…
Rotten with the passage of time,
and lack of care.

Termites eating "Our" democracy,
from the very roots to the high bows.
Crocodiles and alligators,
government entities,
joining forces to rule,
not voted in,
but brought up…
through the ranks.

Tyrants are not born,
they are created in the dark,
by those that are afraid,
and must build a Frankenstein,
to match a Superman.

Wake up,
your party is not well,
it is in the last spasm of complete loss.
Folded by socialism,
betrayed by religions,
Benedict Arnold'ed by Pharaoh,
in favor of outsides.
Not of home at all.
Making way for the elite to rule,
the small
and take the heads...
from the tall.

38) Angels Sing

I hear them,
all the time.
When I pick up my child,
and hold her close,
her breath…
Harps; lovely,
faraway,
and distant.

When I go to my grandmothers,
and clean her kitchen,
all afternoon,
while she teaches me,
how to make,
cornbread and beans…
the right way.
Violins and soft flutes,
as she smoked for 60 years.
She is dying,
My heart is crying,
but the woodwinds are respectful…
of her years, if not my tears.

When I go to my loves grave,
and stand beside the small flag,
I can hear the band,
playing Rock Songs,
favorite one time hits,
and the Star Spangled Banner!
The vocals, on high,
Every word a blessing
to the family,
you left behind.

The freedom to listen,
The freedom to sing,
to laugh and pray,
about everything!

The freedom to sing,
to laugh and pray,
about everything!

An Alliance

The world is calling out,
for a time...
when things the are true,
they are not,
and they should be.

Undetermined,
yet ordained opposites,
facts instead of dreams. .

Lunacy.
the normal...
mental...
path.

Bipolar...
got my scripts.
yesterday.

The weak and the lost,
a band of brothers,
without parents.
a country in denial.

We want phones,
cars, stars,
and all that goes
with it.

We will receive,
exactly,
what we have earned,
and is more than…
deserved.

Perhaps not today,
maybe not tomorrow.
There is no end,
to the tumultuous,
possibility of a future,
where eating
our dogs…
is
normal?

40) The Cane

Not made of candy, but real wood.
It belonged to my father's father,
and his father, before him.

No, they were all good man.
all equally healthy and mostly happy.
The one thing they all had,
that was shared…
Oak.
Fine wood, carved…
hand made,
personally designed,
a project,
to define a legacy.

Freedom.
Purchased with the blood,
of the citizens,
the fathers of sons,
now gone.
The fathers of sons,
that knew sacrifice.
They knew what it was
to be far from home,
and alone.
To protect, all that they cared for,
with all that they had.

Oak.
Solid wood…
 from the Great American Forest.
Grown on a land that still believes,
all have a place.
The weak are not afraid.

They are allowed to offer their worth...
to the community and the society as a whole,
without concern, or even fear.
The lost, are not afraid,
they can pray in public and not be hung.

The heroes, they march down
every street...
Hail to those,
that put others,
before themselves.

The cane.
It is a symbol...
Carved with an eagle at the pummel.
The shaft is inlayed with silver,
copper and precious stones.

It will not break,
Iron is its core.
It is not a disability,
to walk in honor,
for all those that came before.

It is an honor to remember,
we can walk free at all.

41)
The Line

At the store,
there was a sea of people.
Not one or two or a thousand,
drops from heaven,
that never stopped
On a parched land
of holiday cheer.

Shopping lists,
wish lists,
Christmas lists,
and the like,
none to show all that was needed,
but many contained well written,
notes on what was wanted.
What was missing?
And least prominent,
the appreciation of prayer.

It is the first line,
the bottom line,
and every line between.
It is the party line,
the fine line,
and the last line,
you will ever need to read,
in the bible.

They tried to change the season,
the very reason, that we gather.
How can they ever understand,
why we kneel?
how to love…?
this land, our land,
from sea to shinning sea.

You have to have a heart,
a sacrifice of soul.
Believing in something larger,
than self.
God, family, country,
the things that once,
made "us" better,
as a people,
undivided,
unbreakable,
even in our diversity.

Do not let the flies,
Unstable, ruthless
and maniacal…on power,
drunk on dung,
cheat you, me, we,
out of "Our" future!

42) What Party Are You?

Huh?
Does it matter?
Who I voted for?
I am alive,
so it was legal.
I have not been dead,
for thirty years.
Surely that is enough.

If I tell you this or that,
you will condemn me
for the weather.
If I stand for the innocent,
you will strive to make
me ashamed.(or try too)
A common courtesy shared
by many… once.
(empathy for the weak,
kindness for the innocent)
Now only protected and
cherished by a few.
Similar to freedom,
herself.

The fact that I voted,
in the last elections,
should say volumes about
the desperation of the times.
Not that I do not vote,
each and every chance I get,
as I do.
It is a privilege,
and a right…
Thank you to OUR forefathers.

Now…
I find that I am angry,
and I never am.
I find that I am unsure…
and I do not like it.
I want to raise the flag of my country,
and tell my neighbors to do the same,
or perhaps, it will be too late,
to raise anything at all,
including our own children.

Don't badger me as I watch bad things happen.
The people I once trusted for the news,
live on lies and eat dust for dinner,
the truth of their own smoke.
They have jumped ship willingly,
or perhaps meandered away…
Little difference in the end,
to the people they once faithfully served.
Now they take turns, laugh and make jokes,
at the expense of the nation herself.
At the expense of her people,
the ones still left with non-stolen ID's.

The small ones, with small jobs,
like; the postman, the baker, the grocer,
the maker of pots and pans,
the soldier and the officer,
the fireman, and the chief.
The homemaker, the parent,
the pastor and you.

"They" call us names,
and do it still.
"They" repeat gossip and lies,
like it is truth and fact,
gold and silver,
materials to build a crown,
to an unknown as yet…
disguised, evil
in plain,
sight still unclear,
for now.

What party?;
the one that stands for freedom.
the one that stands for the weak.
the one that is not afraid,
and knows, "In God We Trust"
are not just words.

I am an America.
God Bless America.

Amen.

43) Impeach My Peaches

I voted for Donald Trump.
I wanted a change in life.
I wanted to believe,
that my country,
still was the best in the world,
then when the prior
President,
told me (all of us) we,
would never be...
anything
again.

I voted for a life,
that my kids would be happy.
I wanted to make sure,
they could eat,
and sleep, and live,
in peace.
I wanted my signature to count,
a citizen among illegals (above the law).
I wanted my pledge to matter,
to those in charge.

We put them there,
we put them all there,
in the houses on the hill.
We should evict some,
for non payment
of the honor and glory
they promised
in taking the job.

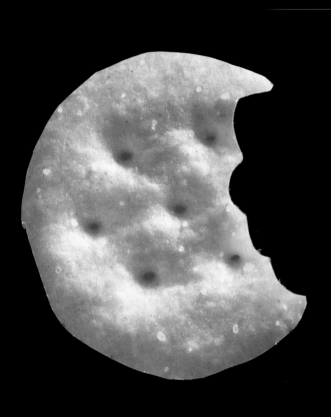

The Koran is not the bible.
America, "In God We Trust"

We need to impeach…
the safe zones, sanctuary cities
"they" created to protect,
"their" own families, and friends,
not ours or yours.
We need to vote,
and make sure who is voting,
has that right.

The only ones against the truth
are those with agendas,
or have already sold out,
to sin and lies.

Historical Outlaws

What, are you talking about?
I am saying that we have a past.
It is full of guns, and law,
and law breakers.
It is full of heroes and villains
and homemakers.

We are America(s).
We stand up,
we do not sit down.
We kneel for God,
and rise to defeat
injustice.

The base of our life,
a collection of men,
full of ideas, for a better world.
One that would incorporate,
all people of the land,
America.

Freedom.
Your skin color
does not matter.
Your are not,
African,
Asian,
Indian,
Or Indian…
Irish or "white" (what ever that means)

The census calls.
Write down the truth.
Make it real, tell it to all.
You, yes you…
and you and you and you.

I am, we are, all of US…
The USA.
Citizens of a country,
That proclaims freedom
more important than death.

45) Stolen Statues

The glory of yesterday,
taken down and destroyed.
Pummeled into dust,
by those that stole their rights,
to be where they are.
They promised good things,
and took away all that
meant anything.
They replaced our heroes
with shadows,
and demanded,
more from us.

Change your religion,
remove your way of life.
Take down all that you care for,
and embrace all that we hate, about you,
and your life, as the truth of our life here…
is now the replacement demanded.

Refusal to integrate, to be part and assimilate,
is sufficient to change the face of asylum.
Invasion is the pretext,
the pretense and the begging…
of war.

Peace, freedom and prosperity,
readily at hand in the country before you.
Why… why…

You ran from all that was,
to all that is,
to make it
the same?
Stupidity is not born,
it is taught.
Everything worth learning
can be learned with an open heart.
War, has no heart at all.

46) Careful Words

Often our mouth(s) is(are)
two steps ahead of,
anything we think.
That is if we think at all.
Which remains to be seen,
or in this case read.

Did I offend you?
How did that happen?
Please don't tell me,
as to hear your voice,
makes my insides crawl.
You "hate" with every breath.
You have written ways,
exactly how lying is okay,
to those unworthy.
You are trained,
and death is a gift
to the weak.
How are we ever going to…
communicate?

You like things I don't.
You hate all that I stand for.
You can not let me alone,
as I must be like you
and do things your way,
even if I am not you.
That is how you plan,
to get to heaven.
Careful,
what you wish for.

Saying things is not a
privilege it is a right.
Odd how the same people
against "it", are using "it".
They weld "it" like a knife,
a sickle, a sword…
cooled and cured
then engraved,
with an evil brand.

47)
Emblazoned...

On their banners!

Numbers placed upon us,
by government officials,
taking money from
foreign countries,
because they can,
because we let them.

Sons and daughters holding jobs,
titles without chores,
money behind closed doors,
cheaters and beaters,
liberals and democrats.

They spend what we give them,
take what they want...
and choose to eliminate
the middle class.

Do you think the poor can support you?
Do you think they give a dam?
They will turn on you and eat you,
Civil war, in this land.

It is not rich that gets richer,
but poor that have a job.
Feed our families,
know that they,
can dream...

You cheat at college,
you are above the law,
you call out others,
for your own sins.
You can be removed...
from office.

The vote!
We will wait.
We are waiting.

Cheat...
and you will know
the sword of defeat.

Black Outside

Soot in the air.
Volcanic ash.
Smoke…
Pollutants…
Politicians.

Choking the life,
out of the people,
all over the world.
It is not a single event.
It is an irrational
chaotic, whirl…
of dirt, and filth…
slung from high places,
where the glass is washed,
daily by monkeys
on ropes above
alligators
that sing,
waiting in the water,
below.

The swamp is a bad place.
Even in the best of weathers.
Beware.

Free Verse, Free Speech, Until it is No longer Free.
Then it will be just Verse.
Not Free at all.
But Censored...beheaded...and then spiked on a pole.
All will cheer, or join the sticks in the sand.

49) Freedom Lost

We had everything.
We tasted the sweetness,
of perfection.
The chance to fly,
The belief, that we…
could reach the stars.
It was real. We could feel their brilliance,
we merely had to want it,
and it was ours.

Dashed to the ground,
by the riot policy.
A huge country, that takes,
no notice of human rights,
frailty of facts,
forced to listen to hate speech.

"Kill them all.
They do not conform.
They look like us, but they are not.
They have been free.
We are not, but we want them
to suffer because we have been cheated.
We don't want to be happy,
We want you to be sad..
and dead.
We want your land, your stuff,
and your offerings…
But we do not want you.
You have been damaged,
by the flag of liberty.
We must gouge out your eyes,
for even seeing a different way.
You are cancer living,
That must be cut away.
Die!"

Still the students hold up their banners.
They throw meaningless insults to dogs.
They decide that it is better,
To live free,
Then to live in tyranny.
God give them hope.
God give them peace.
God give them back,
Their country,
and their way…
of life.

Humbly prayed,
Amen.

50) Heroes Undone

We train men up to go to war.
We train them to fight and kill,
the enemy.
The people…
in foreign and domestic lands,
that have no honor,
and care not for law.

We tell you to shoot,
and maim and knife,
yet when you return,
home…

Some cry that you are changed,
somehow by your actions.
That you are less than citizens,
and even those without I.D.s
planted here by people
that have sold themselves
early to the demons
on the block,
receive a greater due.

God is the judge of all things.
He is the one that matters.
Heavens gates are open wide,
for soldiers
that protect
and serve,
the weak,
the defenseless,
and those
thought without
value at all.

Homage is paid,
for your sacrifice.
The kindest men and women,
the harshest jobs,
the longest hours,
the thankless parades

of "people";
(people: for lack of further description,
prior to my morning coffee)

of do-littler(s),
instead of do-gooder(s),

or even
do-er(s) at all.

51) Protecting the Small

How do people in power rise,
when all they are talking about,
is against everything that can be
remembered…
taught in school?

How can people hold high office,
while the people, the poor around them,
sink ever lower into the embrace of death.

Poverty, and poor houses,
living on the streets,
"stay at home moms" a thing of the past.
Now lucky
 to hold our families together, at all!
What can be said, for living in your car?
The rain is not on your head,
or covering and freezing your feet.

I would call to their empathy,
their sympathy, their idealism, of perfection.
I would remind them,
that I had a job,
I had a wife,
I had family and a life.
Now,
I only have…
a vote,
and you talk
of cheating me still.

How do people in power rise?

52) Appreciation of the Small

Drinking yesterday's coffee,
not throwing it out.
Looking around at the four walls.
They are still there…and I am still here.

Time has lost all meaning.
I had to look at a real calendar.
I have begun to mark off the days,
with giant X's.
They seem somehow comforting,
angry and alienating at times too.

I am holding up.
My family is well.
No one is sick so far.
But we have all been changed.
Not in a small way.
Dramatically.

How many socks does any one person need?
How many shoes, at one time?
How many pens in the drawer?
Paper unwritten upon,
but yet holding the promise of something,
Yet to come…

Take from this,
all of this…
Learn something you did not know before.
Do life differently when next you are…
given the chance to;
say hi to a friend,
hug a loved one,
walk a dog without care.
Plant flowers in the sun,
ride your motorcycle for fun…

53) Ashes

Ashes to ashes, dust to dust…
How many times have we heard this?
on TV, in a play, in a movie…
Have you ever read it in the bible?
The very book of life!
He that made all things,
you, me and the trees,
is the true creator.

Sadly the high in chair,
stare into the dark willingly.
They are using You.
Those in the seat of power.
They speak Your precious word,
to bludgeon others into their own belief.
Not the truth at all,
But a miss-happen, miss-shape-en, explosion,
of warped possibilities all gone wrong,
culminating in a virus that closed down,
the whole world!

Now we watch as our friends pass.
Now we take note,
if not too late;
that people are worth more than money,
that hurting others is a bad thing,
that killing unborn babies is a sin,
and murder is murder…
regardless of reason.

We need to bow are heads,
and know that our prayers…
are desperate.

Judging Others...

It is a kangaroo court,
and the clowns have just arrived.
Dressed in suits and ties,
eating pies.

They think they know best,
they have been put to the test.
Liars on fire...
every "one".

Taking care of a tiger,
that eats cheese crackers...
for breakfast,
can be dangerous.
to you...
and to others.

You are stupid,
with your wishes...
that make fishes die.
You are selfish,
with your demands.
You do not care.
you dare,
to be first,
until the last,
and then fast...

you find,
your hair on fire,
and you are begging
for relief...
from the very
thing, you wanted,
more than life...
itself!

121

Truth Matters

Deplorable.
That is what I am.
That is okay with me.
I work hard,
Have a family.
I support my wife,
and my own kids.
I even adopted a couple…

I am made to pay.
I am made to do what I do not want to do.
I am less than my forefathers,
because I have allowed the works of evil men,
to lead this nation into a bad place.

Under the pretense of fairness,
they have turned my good nature into…
loss and despair.
They have given my hard earned wages,
to those that take and do not give at all.
Those that live off my country, my nation,
and refuse to swear allegiance to her very soul.
"In God We Trust"

They kill babies, in the name of freedom?
I want to scream out, "Whose?"
Murder is murder,
in any dictionary.
You can change the definition in writing,
but the intent of the heart,
will never be different.
Evil is evil.
Then and now.

Voices;
Lifted up in places, far and wide.
Angry and awake, not sleepy anymore.
Robbers go to jail.
Murderers, should never see daylight again.
There are NO Sanctuary cities!
Those that hurt the meek,
shall be placed in the dark,
and forgotten… forever…
Those that helped them,
There is reserved and even better address.
One that best suits the allegiance between
betrayal, deceit, and scum.

The time is getting close at hand,
when truth will no longer be kept silent.
Things will be seen by all,
and choices will be made.

Note the slowness of our citizens,
to listen to authority.
Staying out on the beaches…
Soon, there will also be silence.
And no one…
will tell anyone…
anything…
anymore!

56)
Pineapple Delight

Today is the first day,
The rest will all just follow,
and sometimes get in the way.
There will be good times,
bad times,
out of work,
of out of money,
and even dreadful mistakes.
The kind,
that can not be erased,
even with enough
effort to move a mountain.
There is… or will be,
or even ever has been…
No success.

We eat the finest foods,
green and easily obtained.
The can goods are set aside,
for later.
Grandma taught us…
to be frugal,
even when there was;
plenty.
The truth now,
evident and clear;
"Did we listen?"

Go to church,
stand for the flag.
love thy neighbor,
do the right thing.
in Jesus Holy Name!

Some have forgotten,
Some have chosen to forget.
But the product of all our past
choices have come calling.
They want to be paid for.
They want to be heard.
They want to cause you,
to know that you sold out...
and now,
there is nothing,
left

57) Have You

Ever wondered how it happens?
How the last person stays,
How they make sure, everyone else gets out?

Ever wonder why?
Is that important?
As long as we are safe,
does it really matter who sacrificed;
or more specifically or...
even more importantly what or even when?

The forfeit of something for someone else,
worth a value, more than your own life...
Is resoundingly heard in heaven.
The angels listen closely for all such solemn songs.
Jesus gave his life for all of us.
He stands in the fire beside us...
Even now!

Shout out the shadows,
that gather along the edges of your faith.
"You there... Be afraid!
My God is near and it is you that should fear...
My Lord...He is with me,
and I AM SAFE."

Peace.
That is what they have.
That man that holds the door, for the last to make it through,
the one that gives to others, and does without,
the one that stretches small things, into big differences,
for many at his own expense...

They...
those men...
and women... have peace.

Wash your hands,
Stay inside,
Don't breathe on anyone...
Stay still, at peace and pray.

The Passing of Fear

A mark on the door…

It is so quiet here,
I believe that I can hear a snake,
meandering across the dirt road,
along the backside of the west fence.
Usually he takes his time,
but tonight,
he seems to be…
in a hurry.

"Where are you going slithery one?"
"Where do you think you will be welcome?"

We all need a home.
We all need a place to be.
When the night is darker than thought possible,
and the stars have not come out at all,
bow your head and pray,
there will be a dawn.

The promise of today,
is not the tomorrow…
we dreamed of,
as young and stupid, perhaps foolish children.
Instead it is the one that we deserve,
for doing all that we were told
would hurt us in the end.
Yet, even being warned,
we continued forward…
Ever believing in our own immortality,
rather than the truth of our eternity.

59)

The Mask of Fate

(This poem deals with the Corona Virus. It is very intense.)

My kid's school called.
The college.
They said that there had been...
a national concern; regarding the Sun.
No...

That was not it.
The man said "Corona".
That means crown.

Only the darkness would wear,
an ugly thing made of small bones;
the remains of children unwanted,
and decorated with...
the teeth of the aged.
But Hilter skinned his victims.
They were used to decorate his home.
He preached from the throne of hell.
Assembled at the very base,
of his rule, to shout his cause,
only an echo of the real war,
still raging all around.

The efforts of minor minions...
to disperse the truth,
the holocaust
and all its cost to the Jews,
and the souls of all men,
that still walk the earth then and since.

A dozen tyrants rising and falling,
like the sands and dunes in the desert.
Believing themselves more worthy,
of life and living than the next man. (or woman)
An evil chant,
"children have no worth"
"Old man, give me your money."
What value is anything?
A covenant of good...
or evil?"

Countries killing the voice of their people,
slitting their throats with restrictions,
against the liberties of peace,
and freedoms to worship God, the Father.
His mighty Son.
and...
the Spirit that lives and is real!

The skeleton has climbed,
into the saddle of his steed.
He has lit his sword on fire,
with the oil taken,
gleaned from the glow of lies.
Deceit his favorite game,
his mounts name...
Superstitious!
But no one will care,
they will watch closely as the media,
paints the pictures in bright colors,
that they want the world to see.

The woman in red is in plain sight,
and she is not running at all,
but ready to fight.
She has no weapon...
She has been disarmed.
But they do not understand,
improvising makes her...
more dangerous.

Hail,
the ugly man without a face,
he has no skin... and only bones.
Hail,
though he rides,
he does not walk...
spitting into the waters of the well,
the place all souls drift downward.
Soon even they will see the bottom,
and their hopes will wilt away,
like brittle leaves,
at the end of every season.
Only this one,
will be the last.

Locked in boxes stacked like blocks,
in a giant children's playhouse.
The very air,
drifting in and out of the buildings,
inviting death not only to one,
but whole families by association.
It spreads.
He rides.

The 4th Horseman
And the grave was closely following...
Authority given them over the fourth part of the earth... to kill.
Food shortages and deadly plagues and by the wild beasts of the
earth." —Revelation 6:8.

Angels in Blue

Saints in Green

The hospital is a cold and sterile place.
It is not meant to be...
warm or nice.
It is meant to be a building...
set aside;
to let life win and death,
have no chance at all.

The emergency rooms:
are packed,
now...
all the time.
Coughing,
and gasping can be heard,
not just from the sick,
but by those that attend them...
closely.

Fearlessly nurses, doctors,
and all those involved with care;
move about.
Their dance,
one step ahead of the horseman,
two leaps ahead of tomorrows...
front page news.

What heroes,
shadows of hope...
Smiles offered to strangers,
that can not be comforted by friends,
or family(ies).
All are fearful of the spread,
and more,
the pain and the cost,
of simply being close enough...
to say "goodbye".

61) Storm Front

My voice is quiet.
I have little to say.
I am listening instead…

I can hear birds.
Not a couple, but many.
They are all around.
They are happy.
They are busy.

The wind…
rustling threw, the trees.
I can feel,
the heartbeat…
of my home.
Jesus…
You are here!

Glorious is the day.
Like a farmer,
I count the eggs;
None… broken.
In fact there is abundance!

No one is sick,
no one that I know.
My prayers are for the others,
The ones that I do not know,
that need them desperately.

Lord protect us,
Holy Spirit, breathe…
that we may know;
time is only halted,
not stopped at all.

Yet it is the "pause",
all across the land;
to take a moment and choose,
as the storm ahead,
is still coming,
and it is not,
just a sickness,
It is far more deadly,
and eternal.

62)
Locked In

The walls all around,
are not what is doing me under.
It is not the lack of air,
food or needed sustenance…
It is not the distance,
between the front gate…
and the back.
It is not the water,
which tastes funny,
because it is not filtered…
but straight from the tap,
and hose…
in the garden.

The tomatoes are turning red.
The flowers are blooming.
The dog is still scratching for fleas.

I don't pull the weeds,
instead I invite the bees,
and pray it is not too late,
for pity's sake.

Jesus,
walk with us…
talk to those that will listen.
Those that will not,
we bow are heads,
and know the outcome,
of their tenacious stupidity.

Right before their eyes,
in front of their faces,
Good and evil all around.
The swords of angels…
flashing in the night,
saving the meek from themselves.

This will pass, the saints know.
This is not the last calling.
But it is a trumpet of wisdom…
Take heed, beware, be aware!
Pharaoh was given many chances,
and then none.

63) I Know

I am not afraid.
The list is very long,
of positives and good things.
There is no reason to fear.
That is the number one reason,
not too.
It is a waste of time,
and possible energy,
that would bring us closer...
to a solution.

If you have nothing nice to say,
get on your knees and pray.
If you can not stop talking,
saying the evil that spews forth,
to take away the hope of others,
gag yourself.
If you need help,
that can be arranged.
There is a group forming now,
at the edge of the abyss.

In the thick of things,
when the world is in the same life raft,
the same small dingy...
we must all, stop the individual(s)
poking holes in our safe zone.
Maybe they are immortal,
or so they wish to believe?
Maybe they can not be hurt,
and feel no pain,
born without conscience?

The very old and the very young,
need us now.
All those in the middle,
must learn to grow up.
They must bare the burden...
not felt since our grandparents depression.
Sit next to grandma, let her talk.
Listen closely to grandpa,
before they are gone...
and we are left out here,
without direction.

"Seek God!"
that is what they will say.
With your whole heart,
with your entire soul.
Leave nothing out.

Time is drawing close,
and our breath can be seen in the cold,
the mist of eternity...
for hell is both hot and forever,
and cold with out limits.

64) Father

Father,
I wish I could sing.
I would sing about anything,
... everything...!

Father,
I wish I could write,
I would pen beautiful...
... words... to You...

Father,
I wish I could dance,
I would dance for you...
until the end of days,
and then back again!

Father,
I would humbly pray to You,
... I give You...
... my s..o..u..l...   "whispered"
I pray it has worth to you,
as you are ALL to me...

Father,
please see...
I l..o..v..e.. thee.... "whispered"

Father,
Holy is thy name...
Holy is thy Son,
The Holy One ...
... ...
... ...
...   "whispered"

65) Like A New Day

Every day is, the same...
and not.
I long to go to work.
I have lost my mind?
What a crazy statement.

I used to hate my job.
I used to long to be home.
I am there now.
I am crazy.
I am?

No, it is the world that has gone.
Crazy is just the beginning...
of the line.
The one that we passed
long ago;
in the sand,
in the dirt,
in the hard pack,
in the concrete,
the blacktop,
and our hearts.

We turned the other way.
We laughed at "churchy people".
I checked the news...
I am not the only one.
I am?

My wife is in the kitchen,
making breakfast.
She has a sweet smile on her face...
But I have seen her every visage,
this one is new.
It is different because she is scared.
She cried all night,
as I held her.
I told her it would be...
okay!
I need...
to be strong.
But...

I am?

I pass them by,
unable to confront my loved ones,
with the courage I know they need.
I walk out to the garage,
to my man cave.
I am the head of house.
It says so on my taxes.
But I am afraid.
I am unsure.
I am?

I lock the door,
as I don't want anyone...
to see...
me.
How stupid I will look.
Doubt filling the edges...
of everything,
renewed by jokes and jibes,
lifted up in unison to fit in,
my whole life,
with the crowd.

There inside,
alone,
I am?

I fall to my knees,
weak with the burden of life.
My heart beats faster, and slower.
My mind reels with the things I need to say.
The words I do not have.
What can I do?
Please...
I am?

Utterances, sounds...
fall from my mouth,
but I don't even know exactly in what order,
things made sense and then they did not.
The only truth, the anguish of my heart,
met the horrific suffering of my soul.

He...
came to me.

He...
comforted me.
He...
did not give me,
a spirit of fear.
He...
gave me,
the love of a Shepherd...

I am lost,
I am found,
"I Am" heard me call.

Ask and He will answer, not once... but every time!

66) Fear

It is a very small demon.
It is a tiny monster,
that never stops chewing on;
anything it can get.

It is the one that hides,
and comes home with you.
It hops on while you are;
at the market, the post office,
work, school and even and/or
at church.
Listening to gossip,
over thinking the unimportant,
and by being unfocused on the big...
picture!

God walks with all of us.
Right beside us in the storm.
Lien on Him.
Talk to Him.
He is listening.

Angels around you.
Angels around your family.
Stronger than all others,
soldiers for the King.
Love each other unrelentingly.
Hold each other high.
Give the names of all you love,
to God in the sky!

Rain down drops of hope,
eliminate all dispair.
Let the saints know,
in their hearts...
ever that You,
are THERE!

67) *The End of Nothing*

I am sitting...
waiting and thinking.
Really going crazy,
slowly insane.
I am at home,
trapped. (by discretion)

My guy is in the building.
The big white one,
that no one likes to speak of,
even in solemn low voices;
these days.
A simple operation,
an easy thing to do,
unless the rest of the world,
has stepped off the ledge.

I would like to run to his side,
I would like to fly in
and save... the day!
Or at least bring my parrot,
I would hide him in my purse.
I would let him loose...
and tell him to be quiet,
and not get us thrown out.
As he talks and tells jokes...
for hours.

I would like to bake cupcakes...
for the whole third floor.
Then make them again,
as I messed up,
and he, my guy is on the second.
While I am at it...
I will just keep baking,

until there is no more flower (flour)...
sugar and... or eggs left.

I would like to bring music.
A player or radio,
as I can not sing.
They would thank me,
and be cheerful about it.

Yet...
There is nothing I can do,
except pray.
On my knees,
in my heart,
with soul lifted up...
in nearly inaudible request,
blind sadness,
and grateful knowing;
"I am heard."

I am not sick.
No one I know is sick.
It is not the reason,
I am not at his side.
I believe...
that together,
we are better apart. (That is all of us.)
Fear and depression...
have been given no place.
This will pass.
My guy will be better.
He will come home.

God loves His children.
Be hopeful,
even joyful.
Turn on the lights,
and tell the dark...
be gone!

We have liberty and we stand.
We have freedom,
and we choose to believe.
We are faithful,
and not forgotten.
We know this...
this sickness thing...

Is nothing,
in the
end.

Do not fear... God did not give us a spirit of fear.

68) Windows

This is a time to look out,
and to look in.
First to see around all the edges,
and then back into the mirror.

Time also has windows.
There is a moment...
when you have the chance;
to be bigger than you dreamed,
stronger than you dared,
and more courageous...
in the face of total disaster,
than any hero before.
As this is personal...

The word is rippling
across the land like a flood,
of freshwater.
Drink deeply and know,
we are;
okay,
not starving,
not screaming,
not dying...
but safe.

The lamb was slain.
The Lion will roar.
But he will never forsake
"His" children.
He is returning...

The earth is moving,
quaking and reeling...
The plague is upon the land.
A judgment;
for desecration and denial.

God gives chances,
more than one,
too many to count.
But the warning is real,
and you can feel it now...
everyone!

Prayers today,
lifted up high for all those afraid...
It will be okay. Jesus is real!

69) Explosions in my mind…

I want to compress my head.
It is getting larger.
I am angry…
with,

(a long sigh)
(the gurgle sound of water draining)
(a hushed unspoken whisper)
(an unvoiced, or at least unheard…prayer)

I am so angry I can not say.
You are too, or will be.
The doc say(s) everyone,
will be, sooner or later.

It is not like birth and death.
It is misery and pain.
It is medications,
hospitals,
gowns without backs.
It is pokes and needles,
and drips and piddles…

Another friend,
another room,
same big white building.
This one giving away,
all that she has,
to save…
another.
I am
humbled.

More needles, more pokes,
No jokes, no hoax…
I hate the building painted white.

I want to paint a rainbow.
Not LBGT pride. (get your own colors)
The real one that God made…
The one "they" can not hide.
I want to ask His mercy,
on this stark place,
Fill it with angels,
that we can know Your
Grace!

70) Still Daylight

In the Dark

The days are gathering…
dust,
and so am I.
Not intentionally,
but metaphorically.

I longed to have more time.
I dreamed I could do things;
sort pictures,
send letters,
be creative…
but I find I am staring at the clock,
wondering when next…
I can;
go to the store, for no reason.
go to the movies, because I have not been.
go to a friends, without fear.
Go out…
and be normal again.

What is that?
A place where we had it so good,
that complaining was a right,
or so we thought it to be.
Now we are unclear about our rights at all?
We still have them… yes.
But many are looking to take them away…
forever.

They have lied to us before.
Be cautious and check everything.
Do not take anything at face value.

Black(evil) crickets were singing;
in the deep snow.
No one noticed...
and now they are right inside,
with us.

Lightning

Far in the distance,
There is place,
I long to go.
A place I want to be.
It is nothing like it is here,
there.

How is it different?
How can anything be…
more or less,
except through expectation.

I gather up all that I love,
to give all that I will ever be..
to you.

I want to make sure you know…
that you understand,
there has always been a reason,
for every tomorrow,
and I do not regret yesterday.

Bare with me now,
know that the time is now close,
and you will have to choose;
to leap across the divide…
or even further.

The waters below,
rocks and tides to carry you, me, we, us…
to places far from our homelands.
Instead, fly…
give all that you have,
more than you know…
and dreams will be
exactly what they are supposed to be,
when written down
and recorded…
in history.

The Truth

Jesus, Jesus…
Please,
bless this house,
as I am only,
a small
mouse.

I need you daily,
from sun's bright show,
to moon's bright glow,
in the dead of all that's night…

Thank you for all…
that… You… do.
Thank you far more…
for what I don't know,
You do…

I lift You up…
in my heart,
it is the right way to start;
every day that I draw breath,
until the day of my death.

I know you will say my name,
and I will know of heaven's home,
as all your promises are in the tome.

You are Our Savior King.

No retreat...!
Surrender is not a word.
It is a way of life.
Once taken,
you can rarely un-choose..

Lies to Our Self

I will be okay.
You, she, we, me, us...
are just fine.
All the time,
we talk too much,
and not enough.

Lose weight,
stop smoking,
no joking...
Screaming at the mirror,
on meth, how dare them?
Gathering in my bathroom,
to sing, loudly, obnoxiously,
until the New Day, is old,
again.

The truth,
a story of our own making,
to fit the need of our less than...
ability to make it down the road of life,
without crashing from side to side.

The law,
of accountability, diminished by social war,
terrorism come to live among us,
in a time that living for God,
can get you killed.
When has that ever,
not been the case?

Those without a forever,
long to destroy those that have one,
in a combined will to choose,
suffering for all,
the right motivation,
to commit sin,
in the name of acceptance.

The media, and news,
"ganda" again, the same as before. (propaganda)
There is a knock at the door,
hit the floor,
they have come to take,
the stake from my heart,
and carve the rest into meat,
for the animals, unseen by those...
blind by color and Light.

No fear,
I cheer,
it is the New Year,
I peer into the darkness...
with a flash light.

New and Upcoming Books
Author Information

Hello friends,
Thank you again for buying by book and
helping to support a crazy dreamer.
Other books I offer in print are:

Hope and Holidays
Available Now for Christmas!

This is a wonderful collection of
short stories for the whole family.

Also:
Redneck Mustard Seeds
Available Now in Print

Crazy things my grandparents
taught me. This collection covers just about
everything from fishing to adventuring into the
unknown.
Enjoy!

Award Winning
International Poet
poetrysoup.com/me/AnnFoster
Stop by and join the soup.
You will have the best fun.
Tell them Ann sent you!

So what's next?

Looking for another book…?
I am now working on a treasure hunting book.
Not just any thrift store journal, this is
about the tips and tricks of dealing.
Some topics: reasons to make money,
and some reasons to let go,
at any cost.

More to follow on;

Finding Treasure,
Selling Stuff!
By
A. Foster

Thank you again for your kind readership and support. Please like me, follow me, review me, and pass my name along.

God Bless America!
Keep her strong
and safe
forever.

In Jesus Holy Name.
Amen.

Notes:

Made in the USA
Monee, IL
28 May 2021